jE

jE

CHASE BRANCH LIBRARY
17731 W. SEVEN MILE RD.
DETROIT, MI 48235
578-8002

OCT - - 2001

CH

To my wonderful uncle, Johnny Floyd,
a building man
A. J.

For Jessica Renaud,
who has taught me so much about construction
B. M.

ANGELA JOHNSON

Illustrated by

BARRY MOSER

THE BLUE SKY PRESS
An Imprint of Scholastic Inc. • New York

THOSE BUILDING MEN

Past the ocean waves
and into the woods,
past the plains

and over the mountains,
worked those shadowy
building men—

Our fathers. . . .

Poor and sometimes

from far away,

but looking ahead. . . .

And building it all.

Working from dark till dark,

the fathers. . . .

Digging and hauling,
moving the earth
to connect water.

Those tired fathers
channeling the Erie,
channeling the swamps,
those canal-working men.

The prairies rolled into
mountains' majesty.

But they hammered and laid
hard steel along it.
Cook camps, hard work,
and all of them far from home. . . .

Those railroad workers,

those blue-sky working men.

You can hear the echoes
of the ones who were there
to connect all.

And when the roads came through
with our fathers saying,

"Ain't that something,"
as the trees and mountains
came down.

The fathers' skin burnt in the sun
at the backbreaking work,
but they'd look back and say,
"Ain't that something."
"Yeah, ain't that something."

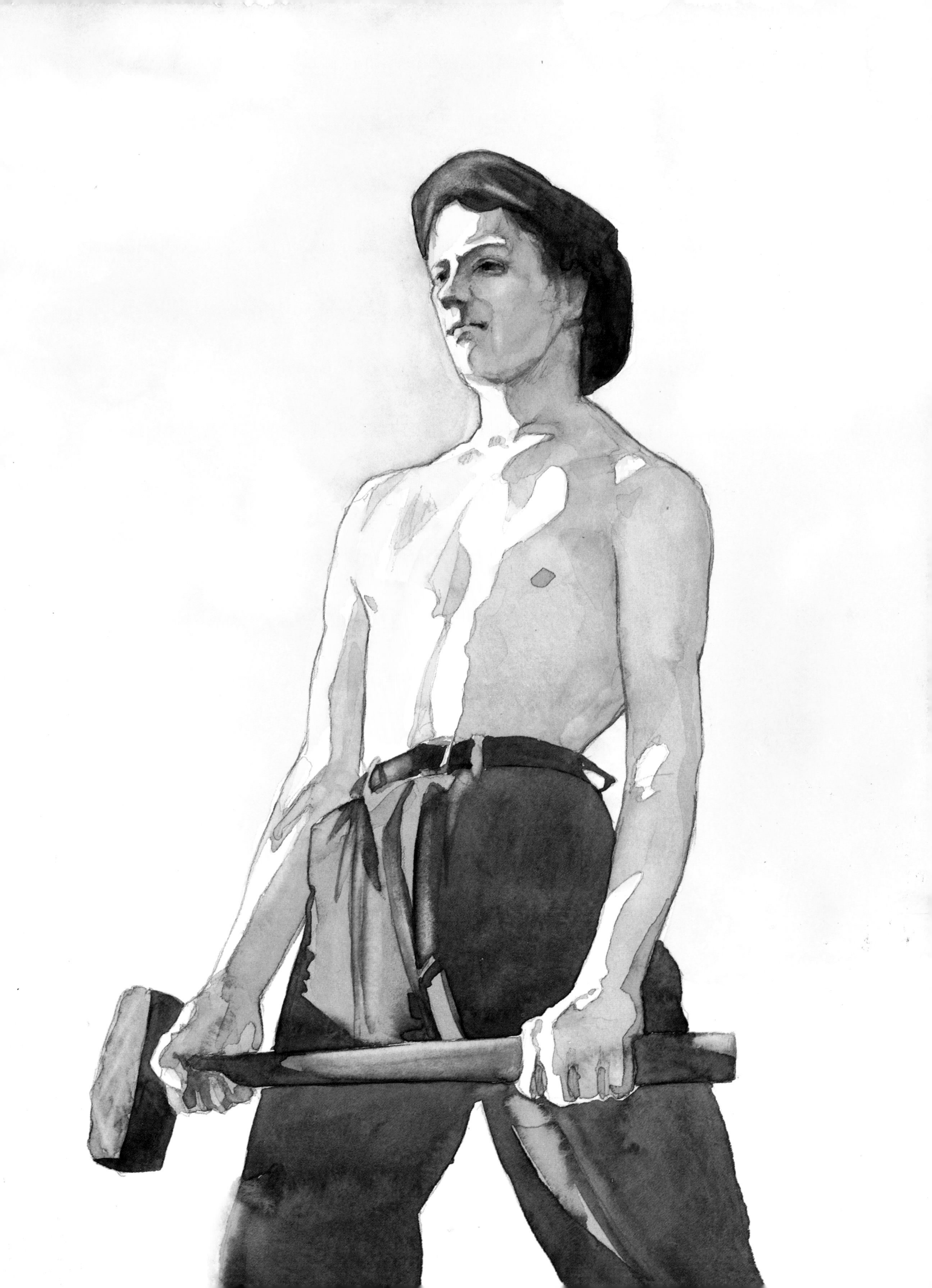

As buildings tower above us,
they tell the tales
of the cities. . . .

They whisper down past it all and say,
"They built us; your fathers.
Walls of steel,
towers tall,
their hands so strong.

“Fearless air climbers,
those fearless air-climbing men.

“And all those sky walkers,
surefooted sky walkers,
native sky walkers.

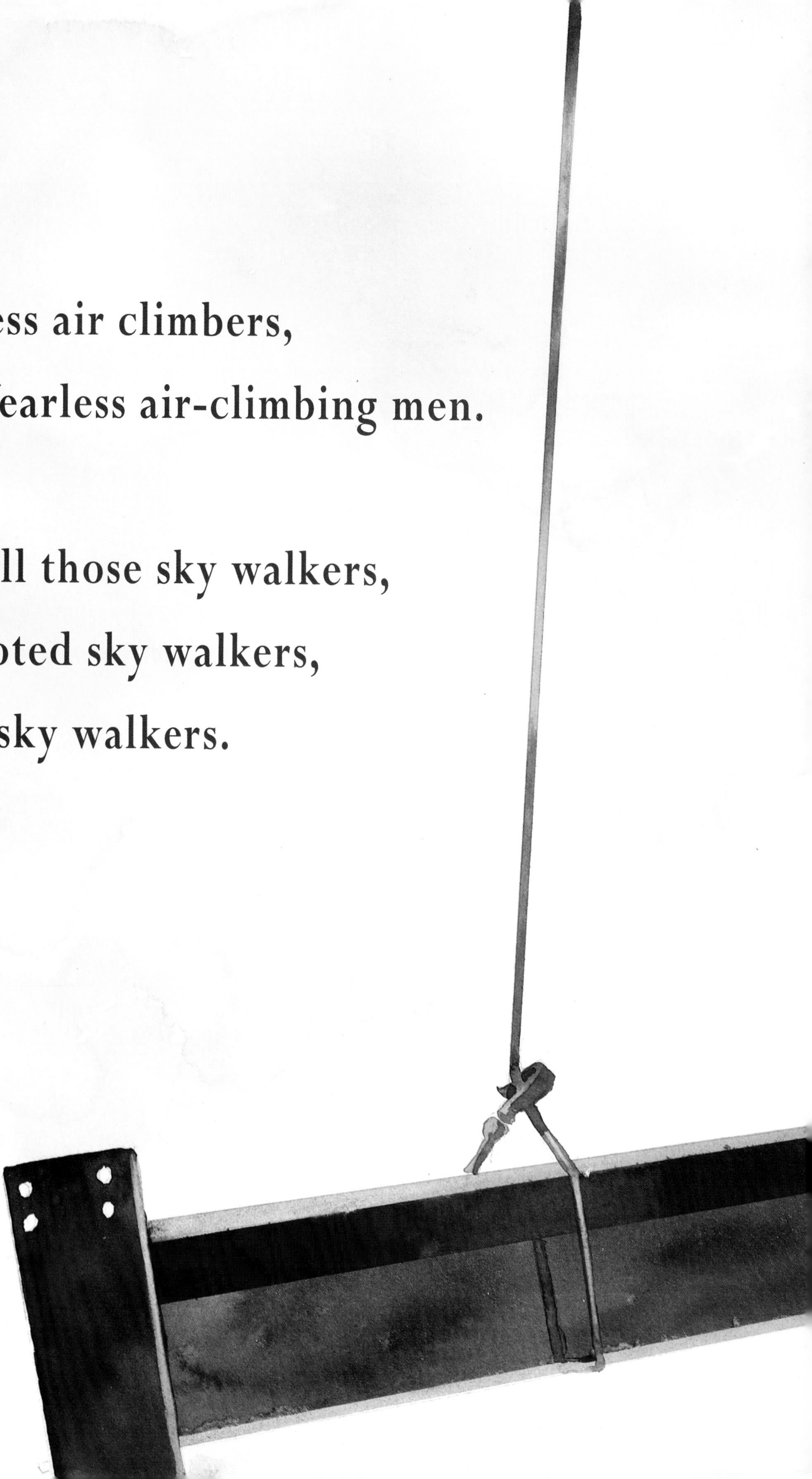

"Bridging, bridges.

"Those steel cables
singing in the wind.
Over it all,
yes, over it all."

Now we look on it all

and remember our fathers.

Those building men.

Those strong,

but now shadowy,

building men.

A Note About this Book

THE POEM AND PICTURES in this book pay tribute to the men who physically labored to build the roads, bridges, railroads, and tall buildings in America. Many of these people told stories that have been passed down orally from generation to generation, and they are a part of our family histories and our multicultural heritage. Women and children also labored along with the men, and in other ways as well. Pushing plows, raising

barns, digging trenches, felling trees, ordinary people from all over the world worked hard to make America their home. And they are still coming.

From Native Americans to Europeans to Asians to Africans who were brought as slaves, those building men have changed the landscape of our continent forever. Their blood, sweat, courage, and tears have left a permanent mark on American history.

THE BLUE SKY PRESS

Text copyright © 2001 by Angela Johnson

Illustrations copyright © 2001 by Barry Moser

All rights reserved.

No part of this publication may be reproduced, or stored in a retrieval system,

or transmitted in any form or by any means, electronic, mechanical, photocopying,

recording, or otherwise, without written permission of the publisher.

For information regarding permission, please write to: Permissions Department,

Scholastic Inc., 555 Broadway, New York, New York 10012.

SCHOLASTIC, THE BLUE SKY PRESS, and associated logos

are trademarks and/or registered trademarks of Scholastic Inc.

Library of Congress catalog card number: 98-005715

ISBN 0-590-66521-9

10 9 8 7 6 5 4 3 2 1 01 02 03 04 05

Printed in Mexico 49

First printing, February 2001

Designed by Barry Moser and Kathleen Westray